A ROCKETFUL
OF SPACE POEMS

POEMS CHOSEN BY JOHN FOSTER

ILLUSTRATED BY KORKY PAUL

D1315599

Frances Lincoln
Children's Books

Contents

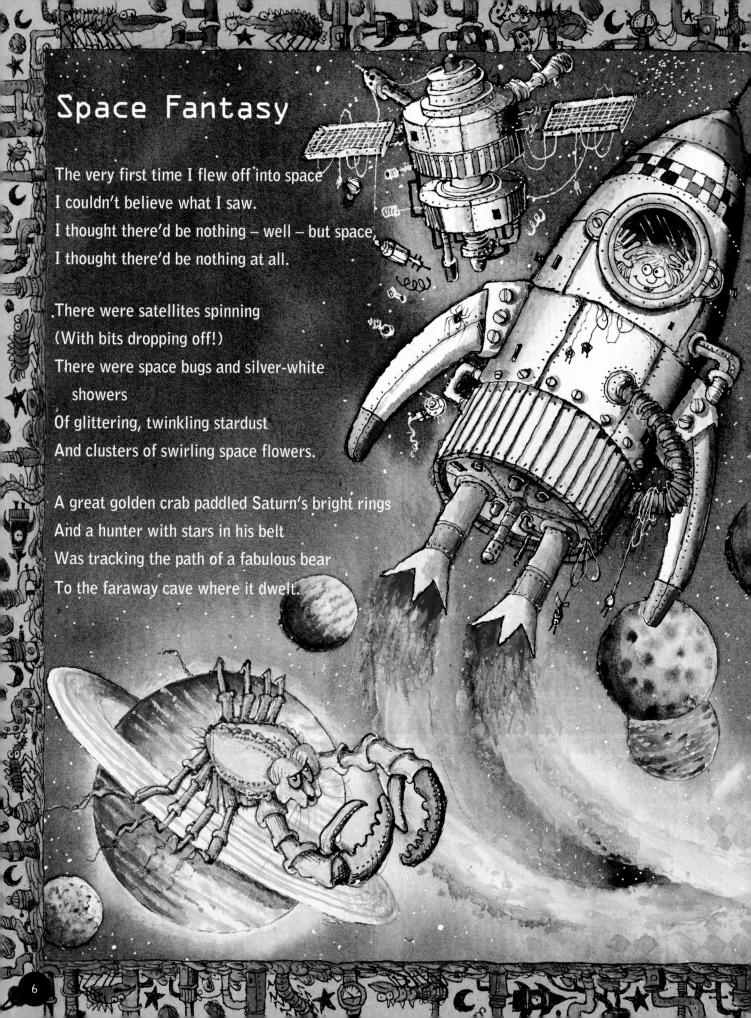

Space Fantasy

The very first time I flew off into space
I couldn't believe what I saw.
I thought there'd be nothing – well – but space,
I thought there'd be nothing at all.

There were satellites spinning
(With bits dropping off!)
There were space bugs and silver-white
    showers
Of glittering, twinkling stardust
And clusters of swirling space flowers.

A great golden crab paddled Saturn's bright rings
And a hunter with stars in his belt
Was tracking the path of a fabulous bear
To the faraway cave where it dwelt.

There were line dancers dressed in silk shirts
    and red boots
Stomping away down on Mars,
There were icicle birds around Neptune
And Plutonians plucking guitars.

Fire snakes flicked along bright curving tracks,
Luminous moonfish swam by
And space horses tossed their manes and neighed
As they galloped the starry skies.

I flew on through galaxies, flew on through time,
Spaced out by the wonders I'd seen.
And no one can say it was all a dream—
No one can say till they've been.

Patricia Leighton

If You Drive to the Moon

If you drive to the moon in your average car,
And you wonder how long the trip is and how far –
Here's the answer. At seventy miles per hour
In the family sedan with its average horsepower,
No skyway patrolmen out cruising for speeders,
No need to feed flying parking meters,
Make sure you pack plenty of outer-space food,
Star-carsickness pills for the high altitude.
Now to get to the moon on the lunar freeways
Will take you...

134 days!

J. Patrick Lewis

Spaceman McTavity

They told him, 'You'll float
as there isn't much gravity.'
Then off to the moon
hurtled Spaceman McTavity.
He jumped from his spaceship,
down to the ground,
and much to his glee
started bouncing around.
'I'm as light as a feather,
I'm lighter than air,'
he sang as he bounded.
'I haven't a care.'

He perched on the craters,
he floated down slopes.
'On Earth,' he said, 'you'd have
to do this with ropes.
In fact, if you tried it,
you'd soon be in trouble
but here on the Moon
I'm as light as a bubble.'
But Spaceman McTavity,
returning from space,
jumped to the ground
and fell flat on his face.

Marian Swinger

'Jump Over the Moon?' the Cow Declared

'Jump over the moon?' the cow declared,
'With a dish and a spoon. Not me.
I need a suit and a rocket ship
And filmed by the BBC.

'I want a roomy capsule stall
For when I blast away.
And an astronaut as a dairymaid
And a bale of meadow hay.'

She gave a twitch of her lazy rump.
'Space travel takes up time.
I certainly don't intend to jump
For a mad old nursery rhyme.'

Max Fatchen

Asteroid Dog

I'm an asteroid dog
And it's boring,
Hurtling through infinite space,
With no little green men I can play with,
And no little green cats I can chase.

I'm an asteroid dog
And it's boring,
With nothing much better to do
Than to watch the stars spin till I'm space sick –
And not even a slipper to chew!

I'm an asteroid dog
And it's boring,
No rabbits, no alleys to prowl,
So I sit all alone on this cold lump of stone
And I howl and I howl and I howl
And I howl and I howl
And I howl and I howl
And I howl and I howl and...
I howl.

Richard Edwards

Turn Left at the Moon

A UFO came down today
At the bottom of our garden.
From a hatch a small red man popped out
And said, 'I beg your pardon.
I'm afraid we've lost our way in space.
Can you put me right for Mars?'
I told him, 'Straight on for the Moon,
Turn left, then through the stars.'
He smiled at me, said, 'Thanks a lot.
Don't mention that you've seen us!'

The trouble is: I got it wrong
And directed him to Venus.

Eric Finney

A Space Odyssey

Percival Pettigrew packed his pyjamas
and parted for Pluto, pausing at Mars.
He steered left at Saturn,
roamed right at Uranus
but missed the last signpost,
got lost in the stars …

Judith Nicholls

Email from the Space Hotel

Hi Mum. Say hello to Janet.

It's really cool on this planet!

The hotel is shaped like a giant wheel

And the manager is a hairy eel.

The receptionist is a flying frog

And the head waiter's a three-tailed dog.

The food is fab. Space-worms are delicious

And the chef says they are quite nutritious.

I'll bring a kilo home for you

And a packet of space spiders too.

My room-mate's an alien called Xim.

I'm getting on really well with him.

We've been on some amazing trips

And piloted our own spaceships.

It was scary but I managed to avoid

Crashing into a passing asteroid.

Got to go now as it's time

For our daily swim in the Pool of Slime.

Then I've a lesson in telepathy

Which my room-mate's teaching me.

Attached some pictures of our visit to the crater.

Must dash. See you later.

Love you loads.

From your son in space, Winston Rhodes.

John Foster

Flurp Blurp

Greetings from the Milky Way!
Seen lots of suns this holiday…
thanks for the comments and concerns
on my album 'Radiation Burns'.
The Big Dipper tour was great – real thrills –
I'm glad I packed my space-sick pills!
Spacebook friends, I need advice,
this Galaxy Tour was sold half price –
can I sue for tour staff being rude
when I mentioned wormholes in my food?
I broke 3 legs on Mars whilst skiing,
3 more on Saturn's rings sightseeing!
Ring spins are fun but I protest
I don't think they've been risk assessed –
it was a rocky ride, alas,
but the planet, close up, was a gas!

Our black hole visit's off as well,
due to a lack of personnel,
they say the alien that ran it's
disappeared with several planets…
Today's a UFO Earth flight
to give them all a nasty fright!
I'm beaming back late afternoon,
update my status very soon,
till then if you're in video mood,
see my channel on AlienTube!
Like · Comment · Share ·
2 minutes ago via spacebook-satellite.

Liz Brownlee

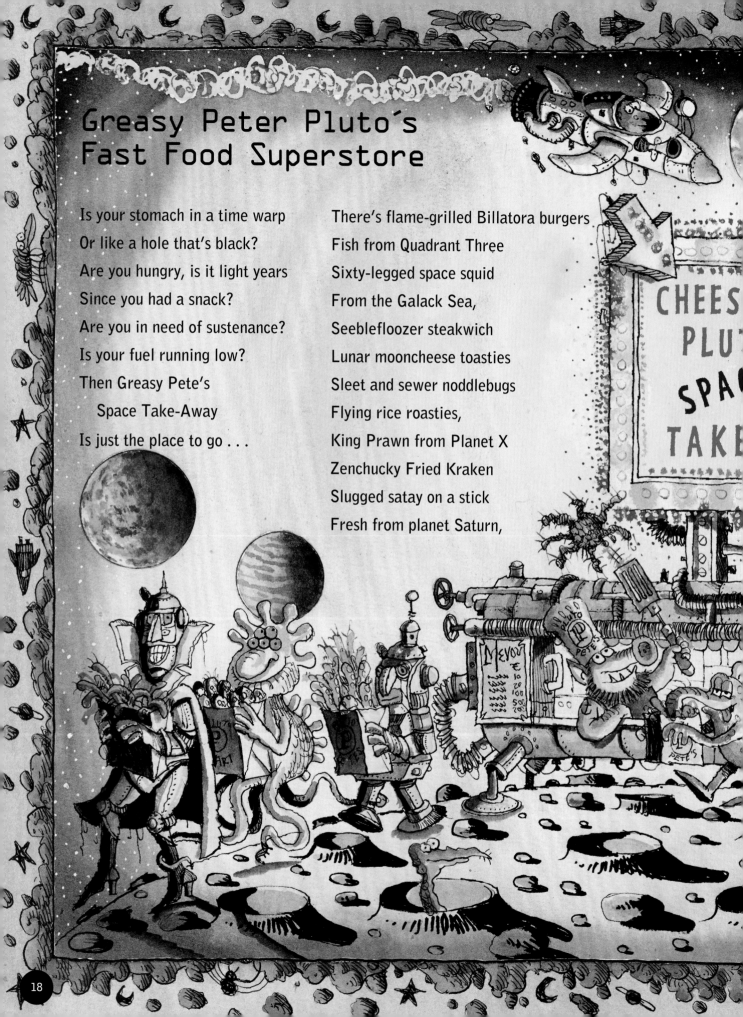

Greasy Peter Pluto's Fast Food Superstore

Is your stomach in a time warp
Or like a hole that's black?
Are you hungry, is it light years
Since you had a snack?
Are you in need of sustenance?
Is your fuel running low?
Then Greasy Pete's
   Space Take-Away
Is just the place to go . . .

There's flame-grilled Billatora burgers
Fish from Quadrant Three
Sixty-legged space squid
From the Galack Sea,
Seeblefloozer steakwich
Lunar mooncheese toasties
Sleet and sewer noddlebugs
Flying rice roasties,
King Prawn from Planet X
Zenchucky Fried Kraken
Slugged satay on a stick
Fresh from planet Saturn,

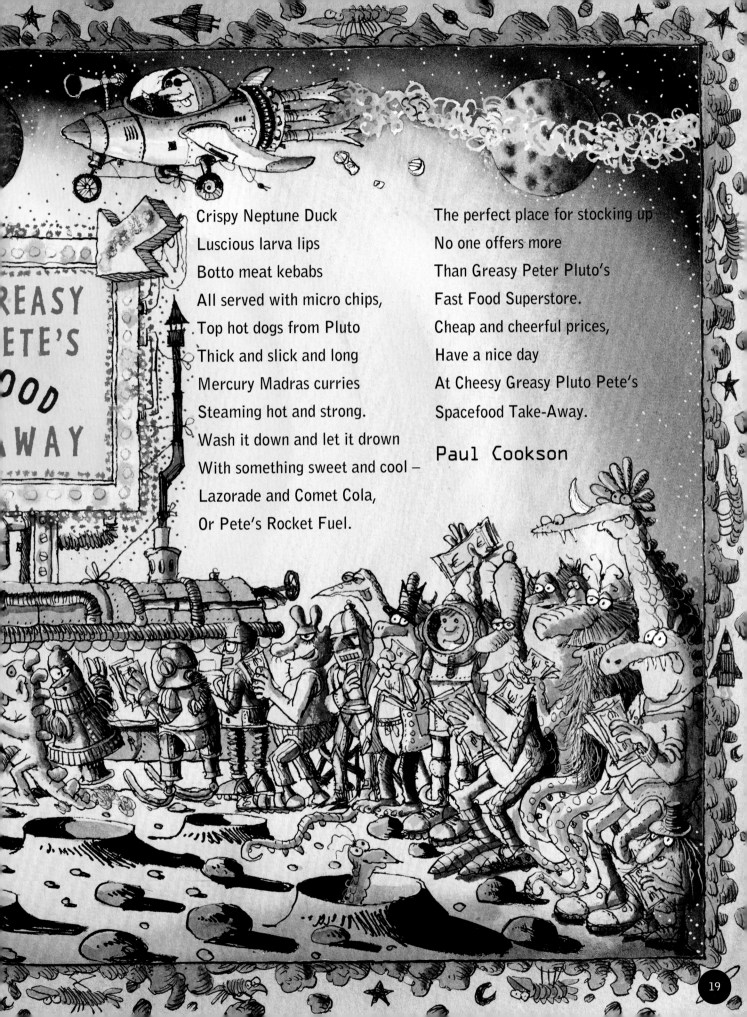

Crispy Neptune Duck
Luscious larva lips
Botto meat kebabs
All served with micro chips,
Top hot dogs from Pluto
Thick and slick and long
Mercury Madras curries
Steaming hot and strong.
Wash it down and let it drown
With something sweet and cool –
Lazorade and Comet Cola,
Or Pete's Rocket Fuel.

The perfect place for stocking up
No one offers more
Than Greasy Peter Pluto's
Fast Food Superstore.
Cheap and cheerful prices,
Have a nice day
At Cheesy Greasy Pluto Pete's
Spacefood Take-Away.

Paul Cookson

Garage Sale in Outer Space

They are having a big sale in Outer Space,
There are wonderful deals to be had.
Like a five-eyed pair of spectacles
For a pound, which isn't bad.

There are supersonic tennis balls,
Black holes in every size,
Plus squirming tendril-cleansing soap.—
Green rocks that harmonize.

A make-up kit for thorny skin,
A robot brain replacer,
Some deep-messaging bubble bath,
A hairy wart eraser.

A flesh-dissolving laser-gun,
Some anti-matter mints,
A bucketful of rocket fuel,
Some Martian red hair rinse.
A flying saucer license plate,
A mountain levitator,
Pet meteors and creeping goop,
A 'Thing' disintegrator.

The sales are great – out of this world;
You'll want to go today.
But just be sure you pack a lunch –
It's a million miles away!

Robert Scotellaro

There Was a Witch

There was a witch who liked to race
Her supersonic broom through space.
At six o'clock last Friday night
She blasted off at speed of light.
She whizzed past Mercury and Mars
Then headed off toward distant stars.
Across the galaxy she sped
A black peaked helmet on her head.
An interstellar traveller, she
Explored the Milky Way with glee.
She chased swift comets here and there.
She watched bright supernovae flare.
She zipped through clouds of cosmic dust.
A witch bewitched by wanderlust.
There was a witch, I'm sad to say,
Flew near a big black hole one day.
It sucked her in just like a bean.
You won't see HER on Halloween!

Elaine Magliaro

The Wizard Said

The Wizard said,
'For my final trick, I will disappear.'
He put a helmet over his face,
Took a rocket from his pocket
And shot off into space.

John Foster

The Worst Monsters in the Universe

The five-fanged Flug of Fizzerflop
eats astronauts and chips
and when you land outside its cave
you'll hear it lick its lips.

If you land on Wobblewig
the seven-headed Vlek
has seven hundred tentacles
to wrap around your neck.

The dreaded Drob of Drooble
is a mighty bird of prey
it mashes spaceships for its lunch
just don't get in its way.

The purple-spotted Swiggle fish
with a sharp and spiky nose
swims around in darkest space
and nibbles at your toes.

The giant ants of Nurdleskip
have long and jagged claws
they'd love to eat you up for tea
beware their crunching jaws.

David Harmer

Supposing

A sinister spacecraft came down on the field
And a hatch in the saucer slid back and revealed –
A nightmare of Martians, all grey and green streaks,
And they each had three legs and three eyes and three beaks!
Then, wobbling weirdly, one came right across
And in Martian demanded to speak to the boss.
So we led him in school to the headmaster's door,
And we knocked, and he opened, and then when he saw –
His eyeballs fell out with a plop on the floor!

Eric Finney

25

Inter-galactic Squibble-ball,

The game is played for ninety moonbeams
   with a break at half-time.

Except on Saturn or Tuesdays.

Each team may have only two dozen players
   at one moment.

With only twenty-two legs between them.

Wingers may have up to fifteen wings.

Goalkeepers are only allowed ten hands/

claws/hooks/pincers/noses.

The pitch must be at least four hundred
   swardblatz long

And at least twelve =thousand
   windycrunchwallops wide.

The goals are always 6.34509808976123
   blipsnottles high

And 17.2308ujyhelp!!!*743901
   bi-squabbles wide.

The net of each goal is to be made of officially
   approved net stuff

the Official Rules

And it is a foul to squander the abblatz
     in the fifteenth quarter
To wybloater the flange or nockadulate
     the grunt
Within five minutes of the second seventh
     or the thirteenth hole.
No player is allowed to be at any time more
     than three octuples from the ground.
Or to trip any other player up.
And there is to be no spitting. Yuk yuk yuk.
Imagine a Snagdongle from Nerk spitting.
Eeeeergh!
Finally, any player between the flange
     or the goal, when the ball is played inside
The groatbucket, is offside. Or not. It depends.
The decisions of all ninety-six referees are final.

David Harmer

Save Our Spaceship

When you're far beyond the solar system
In the vast depths of outer space
And your oxygen supply is running low,
When you have fired off your final missiles
At the closing alien crafts,
When you are at the mercy of the foe,

When your main computer circuit's broken
And you've lost contact with Earth,
When you're hurtling straight towards a black hole,
When your craft's disintegrating slowly,
When the fuel tank's nearly empty
And the capsule's spinning out of control,

When your plight is really desperate,
When you've almost given up hope,
There is only one thing left for you to do.
You must send out the special signal
That only Supergirl can decode
And in the nick of time she'll rescue you.

John Foster

Visitors from Space

Something weird's occurring: something strange in my machine.

My super new screensaver is slithering from the screen!

This just cannot be real, cannot work, computer-wise:

These gruesome, oozesome views I see before my startled eyes!

For a thousand frantic froglets have bounced from my V.D.U.

And they're bopping on the bookshelves and across the bedspread too.

Then loads of warty toads dropped in from some strange cyber-space.

They're croaking close beside me, with a grin on each toad-face.

Some natty newts in spotty suits fell tumbling through the glass

And showers of salamanders, tongues a-flicker as they pass.

A rainbow of chameleons struts slowly to the door
While layers of lizards scurry over ceiling, walls and floor.
No, I did not make one keystroke and I didn't move the mouse
Yet some cyber-phibian menace is filling up my house!
There's shoals of tadpoles making waves within my can of coke.
I'm turning this computer OFF! It's faulty or it's broke.
Yes, I have to turn it OFF and stop this cyber-phibian fright
But the snake that's crawled around my neck
Is squeezing
Much too tight...

Penny Dolan

Bionic Boy

Faster than a bullet
Stronger than an ox
Bionic Boy cuts quite a dash
In vest and day-glow socks.

Wherever evil threatens good
Bionic Boy will go
'Defender of the Universe'
Fighting every foe.

He captures brutal baddies
He puts them behind bars
He saves the Earth from aliens
From Planet Zog and Mars.

He blasts them with his laser gun
Safe in his flame-proof suit
Then loops-the-loop in victory
Propelled by rocket boots.

Having kept the World from harm
Yet always at the ready
He flies off home to his soft warm bed
And snuggles up to teddy.

Richard Caley

Ship Shape Space Ship

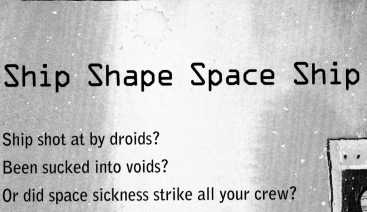

Ship shot at by droids?

Been sucked into voids?

Or did space sickness strike all your crew?

If you're cratered by comets

Or covered in vomit

Let us make your ship shipshape for you.

We'll clean out your spark plugs

And vaporise space bugs,

Check your warp drive is faster than lightning.

We repair dents and holes

And replace toilet rolls

Because Outer Space can be frightening.

Alien ships huge or tiny

Will be shipshape and shiny.

Everyone's spreading the word –

If you want the best

Call S.S.S.S.

Our service is out of your world.

Jane Clarke

BEFORE

AFTER

Texter Terrestrial

One night while I was sleeping
My mobile phone was bleeping
Who was texting me at five past five?
But when I touched the message screen
I saw things I'd never seen
Letters that I did not recognise
Squiggles and some strange designs
Ikons, pictures, wiggly lines
Five eyes on a purple smiley face
Despite all my confusion
I came to the conclusion
I'd received a text from outer space.

Paul Cookson

Dumb Earthling

The poor little Martian was really confused,
He'd landed on Earth by himself,
But he ventured forth bravely and gritted his teeth,
Determined he'd not send for help.

He walked round a corner –
    an Earthling was there,
The Martian looked straight in his eye –
'Take me at once to your leader,' he said.
But the petrol pump didn't reply.

Clive Webster

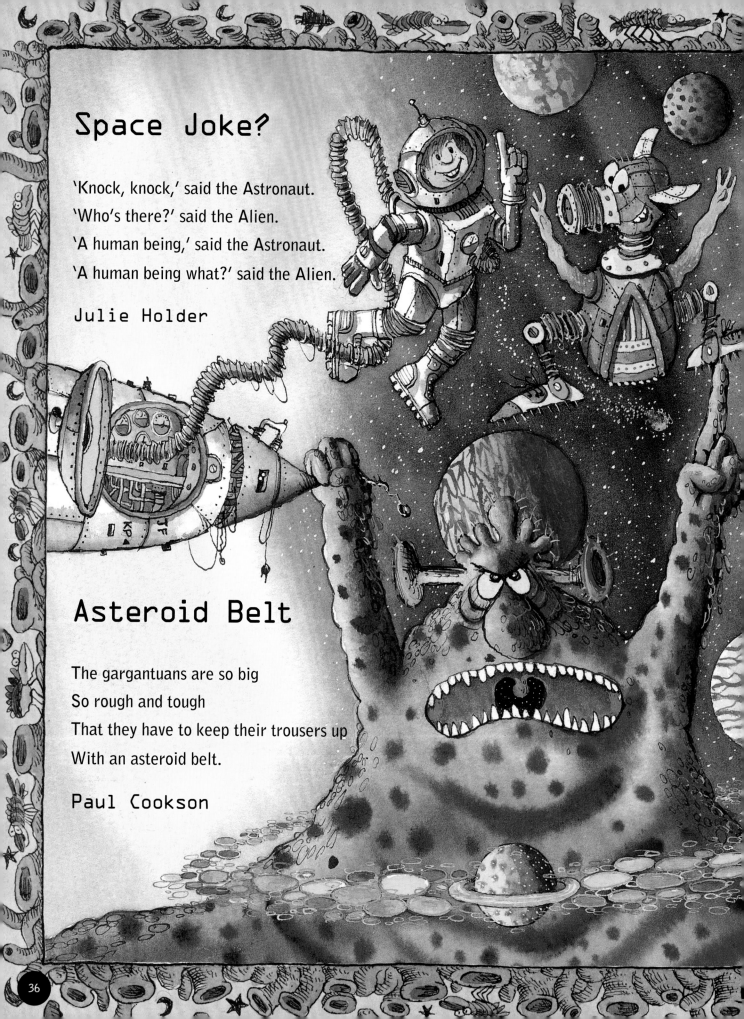

Space Joke?

'Knock, knock,' said the Astronaut.
'Who's there?' said the Alien.
'A human being,' said the Astronaut.
'A human being what?' said the Alien.

Julie Holder

Asteroid Belt

The gargantuans are so big
So rough and tough
That they have to keep their trousers up
With an asteroid belt.

Paul Cookson

Alien Limerick

As on Red Planet, Mars, we alighted,
A very large banner we sighted.
'That's the answer,' I said,
'To why Mars is called **red** .'

It said  MARTIANS ALL L♥VE MAN UNITED

Eric Finney

Space Riddle

I used to be a **P**lanet
But I'd a terrib**L**e shock
When they anno**U**nced
That I was nothing bu**T**
a large lump of r**O**ck.

John Foster

For Evie and Louis – J.F.
To Kate Arden Jannes with love – K.P.

Thank you to Brockwell Nursery and Infant School
for all their help with the endpapers – K.P.

Endpapers by Rosie Wagstaff age 6, Liam Drew age 6,
Jack Wall age 5, and Ava Dymond-Hitchenage 5

JANETTA OTTER-BARRY BOOKS

Acknowledgements

The editor and publisher are grateful for permission to include the following copyright material.

Flurp Burp © 2017 Liz Brownlee; **Bionic Boy** © 2000 Richard Caley, first published in *Superheroes*, chosen by Paul Cookson (Macmillan Children's Books); **Ship Shape Space Ship** © 2001 Jane Clarke, first published in *Aliens Stole My Underpants 2*, chosen by Brian Moses (Macmillan Children's Books); **Greasy Peter Pluto's Fast Food Superstore, Asteroid Belt** and **Texter Terrestrial** all © 2017 Paul Cookson; **Visitors from Space** © 2017 Penny Dolan; **Asteroid Dog** © 1993 Richard Edwards, first published in *Leopards on Mars* (Viking); **'Jump Over the Moon?' the Cow Declared** from *Songs for My Dog and Other People* © 1999 Max Fatchen, included by permission of Wakefield Press; **Turn Left at the Moon, Supposing** and **Alien Limerick** all © 2017 the estate of Eric Finney; **The Wizard Said, Save Our Spaceship, E-Mail from the Space Hotel,** and **Space Riddle** all © 2017 John Foster; **The Worst Monsters in the Universe** and **Inter-galactic Squibble-ball, the Official Rules** both © 2017 David Harmer; **Space Fantasy** © 2017 Patricia Leighton; **If You Drive to the Moon** © 2017 J. Patrick Lewis; **There Was a Witch** © 2017 Elaine Magliaro; **A Space Odyssey** © 2017 Judith Nicholls; **A Garage Sale in Outer Space** © 2017 Robert Scotellaro; **Spaceman McTavity** © 2017 Marian Swinger; **Dumb Earthling** © 2017 Clive Webster;

Every effort has been made to contact copyright holders, but this has not always been possible.
The editor and publisher will be pleased to rectify any omission at the earliest opportunity.

This selection and arrangement copyright © John Foster 2017
Poems copyright © the individual poets
Illustrations copyright © Korky Paul 2017
The right of John Foster and Korky Paul to be identified as the author and illustrator
respectively of this work has been asserted by them in accordance with
the Copyright, Designs and Patents Act, 1988 (United Kingdom).

First published in Great Britain and the USA in 2017 by
Frances Lincoln Children's Books, 74-77 White Lion Street, London N1 4PF
www.quartoknows.com

A catalogue record for this book is available from the British Library.

ISBN 978-1-84780-486-0

Illustrated with watercolour

Printed in China

1 3 5 7 9 8 6 4 2